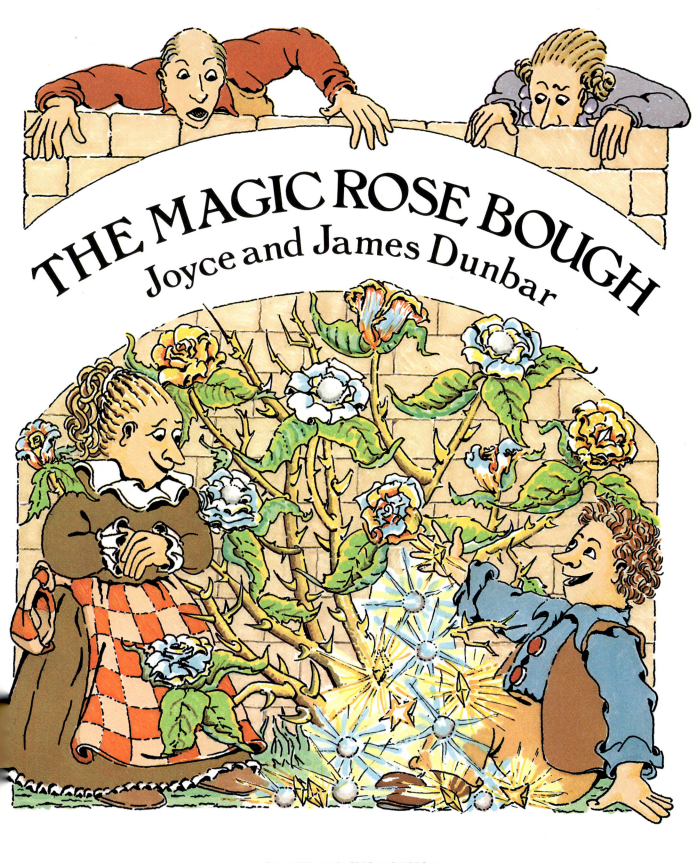

THE MAGIC ROSE BOUGH
Joyce and James Dunbar

HODDER AND STOUGHTON
LONDON SYDNEY AUCKLAND TORONTO

PODSNAP and

Once there was a man called Podsnap who loved his garden more than anything else in the world. He clipped and pruned, weeded and planted, so that his garden was always neat and beautiful.

Podsnap lived next door to Pecksniff, who also loved his garden more than anything else in the world and worked in it just as hard.

PECKSNIFF

Between the two gardens
was a high wall, much too
high to see over.

So Podsnap would admire Pecksniff's
garden from an overlooking window
in his house, while Pecksniff admired
Podsnap's in just the same way. Neither
knew that the other watched;
both were sometimes jealous,
which made both work even harder.

One morning Podsnap went into his garden to approve the work of the day before. How brushed and combed his garden was, how perfumed and how blooming! Then, on his lawn, Podsnap saw an old brown rose bough, prickly with thorns and twisted round with wire.

"What's this?" he said, "on my fresh cut grass? Not mine, that's for sure," and he went to fetch his wife.

"How did this get here?" he asked.

Podsnap's wife looked at the rose bough and then at the wall.

"Pecksniff must have thrown it over," she said. "How else could it get there? Throw it back. Go on. Just you throw it back."

Now, what Podsnap and his wife didn't know was that the broken bough was really a sorcerer's stick that had been buried in the earth for a long, long time, and was full of magic tricks. It was also full of mischief since the sorcerer who controlled it was long since dead.

Without realising, Podsnap had dug it up the day before.

So when Podsnap threw the stick over the wall, it was hardly out of sight when it changed into an old tin tub, and landed in Pecksniff's garden.

"What's this?" said Pecksniff, when he saw the old tin tub in the middle of his lawn. "Not mine, that's for sure," and he went to fetch his wife. "Is this your tub?" he asked.

"What would I want with a mucky old tub?" said Pecksniff's wife. "Podsnap must have chucked it over. Chuck it back. Go on. Just you chuck it back."

On its way over the wall, however, the sorcerer's stick changed itself from an old tin tub into a rotten wooden wheel, which crashed into a flower bed.

"That settles that!" said Pecksniff.
"That will show them what's what," said his wife.
But it did no such thing…

For Podsnap, who was furious, threw the rotten wooden wheel back over the wall, where it landed as . . .

…a broken hat stand!

Pecksniff hopped about with anger.

"See this!" he raged, "in my garden! And look what it's done to my lupins!"

And he threw back the broken hat-stand, where it landed as…

. . . a sack of stones!

"Whatever next?" yelled Podsnap, when he saw his very best shrub squashed flat. "He can keep his rubbish to himself!"

And he threw back the sack of stones, which landed as . . .

... a stinking feather mattress!

And so it went on for several days; the sorcerer's stick changing itself from one thing to another and enjoying itself mightily.

Finally, when it had changed itself into a rusty iron rod, Pecksniff threw it back with such force that it landed like a spear in the the ground and was a rose bough again.

When Podsnap found it, he angrily tried to pull it up.
He tore and tugged but the sorcerer's stick cried out:

"Let me go! Leave me be!
Cursed be the one that kills a tree!"

which made Podsnap jump back
in astonishment.

Then he saw that growing
from the base of the old brown
rose bough was a golden shoot,
such as he had never seen
growing before.

He fetched his wife to look at it, by which time there were two golden shoots.

"Good gracious!" said his wife, with her eyes popping wide. "But what if Pecksniff tries to claim it back?"

"That's a thought," said Podsnap, "though I don't know what's to be done about it."

"I do," said the wife. "Just listen," and she called to Pecksniff over the wall until he was obliged to answer.

"Pecksniff," said Podsnap's wife, "You know that old branch you threw into our garden – are you sure you wouldn't like to have it back?"

"I never threw any such thing," replied Pecksniff, and indeed he hadn't, just an old tin tub, a broken hat-stand, a stinking feather mattress, a rusty iron rod and other things besides. "Just keep your rubbish to yourself."

Podsnap and his wife fell about laughing as the rose bough grew more golden shoots.

And more and more, and then gold and silver roses that bloomed to perfection. Whenever Podsnap's wife cut a rose, two appeared in its place, so that never was a rose tree of such extravagant beauty ever seen before.

The rain that fell upon this rose tree turned straight away to diamonds, the dew to shining pearls, which Podsnap and his wife gathered up hastily and stored in tin trunks in the cellar.

Pecksniff was so mad! So was Pecksniff's wife. From their upstairs window, and even from their garden, they could see the magnificent tree.

They were so envious that Pecksniff no longer bothered with his own garden, for he was too busy working out ways of destroying the wonderful tree.

First he tried to bribe two rats.

"Eat away at the rose tree's roots," he said, "and I shall reward you handsomely."

But no sooner had the rats begun to gnaw than their teeth turned to gold and their whiskers to silver.

"Rats!" they exclaimed as they looked at each other, "with golden teeth and silver whiskers! This *is* a handsome reward!"

The rats ran back to Pecksniff, bristling with delight.
"Just think," they said, "we shall have twenty wives apiece!"

Next Pecksniff sent a grey-winged moth to lay its eggs
on the rose tree, so that its grubs would
eat away at its heart.

But no sooner had the moth settled on the tree
than it turned into a gilded butterfly, and flew
proudly away to show itself off.

Pecksniff raged; Podsnap grew rich.
The rose tree went on growing.

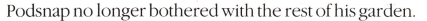

Podsnap no longer bothered with the rest of his garden.

"What is the point?" he said to his wife, "when we have a rose tree like this that grows and blooms whatever happens?"
But he wished he had more to do.

"You are right, husband," said Podsnap's wife, and why should I bother to do any work when there are diamonds and pearls to collect?"
But she wished she had more to do.

Pecksniff mixed a potion, full of pests and fungi, and threw it over the wall. But the wind blew it back into his own garden, which sickened something terrible.

Pecksniff's garden turned into a wilderness and, except for the rose tree, so did Podsnap's.

"Podsnap," said Podsnap's wife one day, "that rose tree is growing over the wall. Pecksniff and his wife might pick the roses and steal the diamonds and pearls."

"That's a thought," answered Podsnap, "but I don't see what's to be done about it."

"I do," said his wife. "We must move the tree to the middle of the garden."

"No, wife," said Podsnap, "we mustn't disturb a growing tree. It would die."

"Rot!" said Podsnap's wife, "it's more likely to die cramped up against the wall."

So Podsnap was persuaded.

He began to dig and his spade struck a root. The rose tree cried out:

"Let me go! Leave me be!"

"Did you hear that?" said Podsnap.

"I trod upon a thorn and cried out," answered the wife, "Carry on."

Podsnap's spade once more struck a root.

The rose tree cried out:

"Let me go! Leave me be!"

"Did you hear that?" said Podsnap

"I was stung by a bee and cried out," answered the wife. "Carry on."

So Podsnap pulled at the tree which shrieked,

"Let me go! Leave me be!"

"Did you hear that?" said Podsnap.

"A bird pecked my hair and made me scream," answered the wife. "Carry on."

Podsnap pulled harder. The tree came out of the ground.
In a minute the rose tree turned to green,
its blooms to plain white and ordinary yellow.
Podsnap and his wife watched with amazement.
In another minute the blooms all fell and faded,
the leaves withered and dried.

Pecksniff and his wife,
from their overlooking window,
watched with glee.

Soon, nothing remained but a
brown old rose bough, prickly
with thorns, twisted
round with wire.

"Never mind," said Podsnap.
"We still have all the dewdrop pearls
and diamond rain."

But when they ran into the house and looked in the tin trunks in the cellar, they found not a single pearl nor a single diamond, just a slop of water, which is what they first had been. Podsnap shook and his wife went wild.

Pecksniff grinned and his wife danced a jig.

Next day, they all looked at the jungles that had once been lovely gardens.

"Tomorrow I shall do some weeding," said Podsnap with a sigh.

"Tomorrow I shall dig," said Pecksniff.
"Tomorrow I shall take some ice to Podsnap's wife,"
said Pecksniff's wife, "to help cool her head."

And somewhere, in two rat holes, forty rat wives
quarrelled with their husbands.

"Where's your golden teeth? Where's your
silver whiskers? You're just common old rats,
not fit for us at all."

As for the old brown rose bough – it went looking
elsewhere for mischief – so watch out!

British Library Cataloguing in Publication Data

Dunbar, Joyce
 The magic rose bough.
 I. Title   II. Dunbar, James
 823'.914[J]   PZ7

 ISBN 0-340-34833-X

First published 1984

Published by Hodder and Stoughton Children's Books,
a division of Hodder and Stoughton Ltd,
Mill Road, Dunton Green, Sevenoaks, Kent TN13 2YJ

Printed in Hong Kong by Colorcraft Ltd